HEAVEN SENT

MICHELLE ROMANO

HEAVEN SENT

Cover Design: Sue Thomson: fiverr.com/suethomson
Ch. Image: Sue Thomson: fiverr.com/suethomson
Format Design: Dawn Baca: fiverr.com/dawnbaca
Special thanks to author Rhea Morrigan (RheaMorrigan.com) who helped to edit this novelette. Her insight was invaluable.

✾ Formatted with Vellum

DEDICATION

Mary Lou,
my friend in Heaven, 1942 — 2018

PROLOGUE

*M*y pulse raced as I sat on the couch, hands clenched, waiting for Evie. I had a secret to tell her—one she should've known a year ago.

Gripping my cane, I hobbled to the front window, eager to see if she had arrived. Despite our thirty-year age gap, we had become best friends: kindred souls, bound by long walks, laughter, and heart-to-hearts that never felt forced.

When I turned around, my vision zeroed in on the shiny, sunlit zipper of my workout bag that lay slouched by the door, untouched. I hadn't bothered to put it away after my gym membership lapsed.

I sighed.

Pain had halted my routines, except for visits with Evie, but since she was finishing out the school year, we hadn't seen each other much.

I smiled at a photo of us eating ice cream on a road trip last summer. We laughed until we cried, trading stories that were too absurd to be true. I loved listening to her talk; it always brought us closer. She could tell me anything, and I had told her everything. Until now.

This secret was different: not funny, light, or easy. It was heavy, and I didn't know how she'd take it. *Would it change everything between us?*

A sharp, stabbing pain ripped through my chest, and my body trembled. Sweat coated my forehead. I stumbled back onto the sofa, an invisible weight crushing my lungs. Last year, Dr. Grace said that I'd eventually feel this way.

My gaze latched onto a photo of Evie and me at the candy store, and gradually, my pulse calmed.

These sensations were worse now than they had been three years ago when Crossroads Middle School forced me to resign. It had been my second home, my whole world, but they didn't have the funds to keep me. That's what they said, but I knew better. Using the computer had become too difficult, and other tasks slowed me down.

My heart still ached at not seeing Evie every day.

The slam of a car door interrupted my thoughts.

She had arrived.

1

EVIE

a chill crept up my spine, and I shuddered despite the summer's warmth. *God, I hope everything is okay.*

Lou lived on the corner of Trinity Lane in a neighborhood dotted with manicured lawns and vibrant gardens. Her gray, two-story stucco home stood in stark contrast with its vine-tangled walls and weed-infested flowerbeds.

As I approached the front step, the door flung open.

I grinned, trying to shake the unease coiling in my chest. "Hi, Lou. How are you?"

"Well…" Her eyes flicked to a dying birch tree.

"Yes?" I sang, hoping to coax a smile, but her gaze, heavy with sorrow, didn't meet mine.

"Are you all right?" I asked, noticing Lou hadn't brushed her bright red hair and wasn't wearing her sparkly green hat.

"I could be better." Her face tightened.

My hand fidgeted with the hem of my shirt. "What happened?"

She didn't answer. Instead, she turned and led me into the living room.

Vintage plates and delicate glassware covered nearly every surface, while porcelain dolls lounged on an armchair. Above the white-painted mantel, a large mirror reflected the room's controlled chaos. A row of tiny glass figurines—animals and children—lined the ledge beneath. The distinct tick of the grandfather clock echoed in the stillness.

Lou sat in a chair and cleared her throat, drawing my attention. "You should sit."

I sank into the couch, dread creeping over me.

"I need to tell you something," she began, her voice unsteady. "My doctor said…"

My stomach twisted with fear. *Oh no, this doesn't sound good.*

She stared at the floor. "I have breast cancer."

Time stopped.

The room faded, and the walls closed in as my mind raced back to when we had met.

It was my first day on the job at Crossroads Middle School in our small town of Mercy, Minnesota. An older woman stood from her desk and walked over to the counter, her lanyard of keys jingling with each step. In the sweetest voice, she asked, "How can I help you, dear?"

"I'm the new social worker. My name's Evie," I said, stretching the e-sound at the end of my name.

"Glad to meet you. I'm Louise—Lou for short. You're going to love it here!" She beamed.

In one of our earliest conversations, Lou told me her parents had passed, and her friends had moved out of state. I didn't have family or many friends either, so we became family—me, the daughter she always wanted, and Lou, the mother I always needed.

Lou's whimper brought me back to the room.

"Cancer?" I whispered, disbelief thick in my voice. *She's only seventy, still so young. Please, God, don't take her from me.*

Lou reached for a Kleenex from the table. "I've been in pain for months—I lost track of time..."

My jaw dropped open.

She added, "I hate going to the clinic, so I didn't go until the pain was unbearable. That day, my doctor broke the news to me. I'm sorry for not telling you last year."

Last year? Why am I just finding this out? We're best

friends, and we tell each other everything. My heart shattered as questions swirled. *Is she going to die?* Tears blurred my vision as I struggled to speak.

When I didn't respond, Lou's voice cracked. "I didn't want to...burden you...or believe it was true."

"You'll never be a burden." Guilt bloomed within. *Why hadn't I seen her more often, and how had I missed signs of her suffering?*

Lou studied me quietly, then said, "I've felt worse these past few weeks. I hurt all over. Some days, I can hardly move. That's why I needed to tell you now."

I went over to her, and she fell into my arms. Holding her tight, I didn't want to let go. I cried, bracing myself for what could come next.

When she pulled away, we sat together again. My chin trembled, and I asked, "Have you considered...chemo? Medication? Is it reversible? It's not terminal, is it?"

2

LOU

The words caught in my throat, but I forced them out. "Unfortunately, it's too advanced. I'm taking medication, and my hair is thinning." My hand flew to my head. *Rats! I forgot to put on my hat.*

Evie stared at me, tears spilling over. "Are you seeing an oncologist?"

"Yes, and I've been going to weekly appointments. Sometimes, they run scans to monitor how I'm doing."

Evie slowly shook her head. "I can't believe you're going through this."

"I know. I expected to live longer. I wanted to see you get married and raise a family. I didn't want you to feel abandoned again."

"Don't talk like that. You can beat this. You're a strong woman," Evie said, wiping her eyes.

I reached out to hold her, and she clung to me. We hugged for a long while. Her whimpers vibrated against my chest, and it was gut-wrenching. If I could just hold her forever, maybe nothing would change, and we'd always be together.

Eventually, Evie pulled away, got a tissue, and dabbed her swollen eyes. "I know this is out of our control. All I want is to spend time with you."

"I want that, too." My heart broke at the thought of my fatigue and illness separating us. I swallowed hard, feeling the dryness settle in my mouth. "I'm going to get us some water."

As I stood and reached for my cane, my legs buckled. I gripped the chair and narrowly avoided a face plant.

Evie rushed to my side. "Are you okay?" She helped lower me back onto the couch.

"Oh my. I don't know what just happened. I was fine, and then I wasn't." My breath hitched. *Is the cancer causing this?*

Evie's brow furrowed, a frown tugging at her lips. "Is it okay if I get us some water?"

"Yes." I exhaled deeply. "Thank you, dear. I'm so glad you're here."

After a couple of minutes, she handed me a glass and sat beside me.

"Today has been draining," I admitted. "And having cancer is scary." *I hate being sick, and talking about it makes my skin crawl.*

Evie's eyes softened with understanding. "I can't imagine how you're feeling, but I'm so glad you told me." She gently took my hand. "What do you need right now?"

I hesitated, then asked, "Can you take me to my appointment next week?"

"Of course, and I'd like to drive you to your other appointments, too." She paused. "It breaks my heart to see you go through this, especially after losing your sister just three years ago."

I frowned. "I have a feeling I'm following in her footsteps."

"Let's not go there. One day at a time, okay? You can lean on me. Whatever you need, I'm here," she said.

"Thank you, dear. That means a lot." I yawned. "I need to rest."

"Okay, but I'd like to see you tomorrow, and the next day, and the next, and—" Evie's eyes danced with hope.

"Slow down. We have time. I'll see you in a few

days and then next week for my doctor's appointment. If something happens, I'll call you." I sighed, my emotions settling. I'd had enough excitement for one day.

Evie hesitated, then stood. "Is there anything else I can do for you?"

I shook my head. "No thanks. I love you."

"I love you, too." Evie bent down and kissed my cheek.

As the door clicked shut behind her, a thread of worry pulled at my chest. *Who'll take care of her when I can't?*

I grabbed my cane, stood, and went into the kitchen. Unopened treats lined the counter. A faint smile tugged at my lips as I glanced at the smoke alarm above. It was quiet now, unlike the other day when it wouldn't stop blaring. The cake I'd made caught fire in the oven. I called the emergency number, and then the fire went out, but three firefighters still came over. I handed each a can of Fresca and a pack of my favorite candy, Chuckles. Their faces lit up like kids at a sweet shop. This memory filled me with joy.

Now, I craved a sugar fix. A slice of vanilla frosted cake sat on the counter, and I gave in to the temptation.

As I savored each bite, my mind drifted back to last month's ice cream adventure with Evie. We'd found ourselves at a sun-drenched picnic table in the park, the golden light filtering through the trees. We ordered vanilla cones with rainbow sprinkles, expecting the usual dip—but our sprinkles came in two miniature paper cups. The sight struck us as hilariously absurd, and we burst into laughter that started deep in our bellies and rolled on until tears sparkled in our eyes.

That moment felt like the world had paused just for us.

A tear slipped down my cheek as my heart clenched, not knowing how much time I had left to laugh with Evie.

3

EVIE

*L*ou had cancer. I couldn't shake it—it was only a matter of time before I'd lose her.

At home, I lay down and prayed. *God, my life hasn't been easy. I've always felt You near, and this summer I was hoping to draw even closer. But now, Lou...please help her.*

Tears lulled me to sleep, quieting my thoughts. When I awoke an hour later, I remembered Lou's illness, and sobs rose, making it hard to breathe. I clutched my pillow, its dampness cold against my skin, and drifted back into a restless sleep.

The next morning, I wanted to stay in bed all day, but I had promised to volunteer at Pete's Bike Shop. Lou and I often did things like that together, but last week, she said she couldn't go. I hadn't understood until now.

I forced myself up, dressed, and drove into Mercy. The morning was too bright. People were strolling down Main Street, laughing and shopping as if nothing had changed. Tears caught in my throat. *It's so unfair how life keeps moving, even though my best friend is dying.*

I pulled up to the bike shop and walked inside. A bell startled me.

"Good morning, you must be Evie," an old man said in a deep, friendly voice.

I hesitated. "Yes, I'm here to volunteer."

"I'm Pete. Thank you for coming. We need all the help we can get." He gestured for me to follow him.

At the back of the shop, he said, "We repair bikes to give to kids who need them. Ever done anything like that?"

"No, but I'm a fast learner."

The bell rang again. "That must be our other volunteer, your sidekick." Pete winked and left.

I peeked into a mirror on the wall, catching my reflection. My face was pale and my eyes droopy, like I hadn't slept in days.

I took a deep breath. *First impressions matter.*

Maybe Lou will bounce back, and we can come here together. My fingertips grazed a pink basket attached to a child's bike.

"Evie, this is Gabriel," Pete said.

I turned, dazed, my thoughts still clouded by Lou's news, but something about the man in front of me piqued my interest. Gabriel was tall, handsome, and fit.

"Hello," he said, his gaze meeting mine, steady, searching, almost holy. It wasn't just his eyes, though warm and piercing; it felt like he could see past the sorrow tangled inside me. For a breathless second, it was as if our souls touched, something eternal sparking between us.

"Ahem," Pete interjected, breaking the moment. "Let's get you guys to work. Members of our church donated all of these bikes, and today, three will go to kids who need them. You'll be adding accessories."

I caught myself looking at Gabriel. He seemed to be in his early forties, around my age. As he helped Pete, his dark red shirt hugged his body, showcasing his muscles. He bent down to grab a fallen bike, and a Trinity symbol dangled from his neck. It reminded me of Lou's street, and a rush of sadness hit me.

"Um, is there a restroom here?" I asked, my eyes misting.

Pete nodded, pointing to the front of the store.

"I'll be right back," I said, walking away.

When I was alone, tears trickled down my cheeks. I blew my nose, regaining control of my emotions so I could help out and then go home. Afterward, I went back to hear the instructions.

Pete noticed my expression and hesitated before saying, "There are piles of bells and baskets everywhere, so choose whatever you want to make these babies shine." He retrieved tools and cloths and handed them to us. "I need to work up front, so let me know if you guys need anything."

As he walked away, I rubbed my watery eyes.

Gabriel glanced at me. "Are you all right?"

"Oh, sorry, my best friend is sick, and I've been trying to put on a brave face," I said, feeling silly disclosing this to a stranger.

"Please don't apologize. I understand."

I cleared my throat. "Have you volunteered here before?"

Gabriel grabbed a wrench, and his biceps flexed beneath his shirt, pulling my attention. "No, this is my first time."

"Me too. What can I do to help?"

Gabriel smiled. "Once I unscrew these nuts, we can attach some pretty baskets. Could you choose a few from that large pile?"

I wiped my moist hands on my pants. "Sure."

As he whistled, fixing the first bike, a green, shimmery stream of energy glided along his silhouette. While I stared at the light, a wave of contentment grounded me, and I couldn't move. I breathed out a heavy sigh and closed my eyes. When I opened them, his aura disappeared.

"Well, what are you waiting for?" Gabriel teased, catching me staring at him.

Flustered, I said, "Right. The accessories." I turned around to choose blue, green, and yellow baskets, along with three silver bells.

"Okay, hold the blue basket here." He motioned to the handlebars. "Then I'll screw it on."

As Gabriel leaned closer, hints of sage and cedarwood wrapped around me, making my heart flutter. His hand brushed mine, and a ripple of goosebumps traveled up my arm.

We continued attaching the remaining baskets and bells and wiping them clean. The rhythmic work was calming, though the occasional touch of Gabriel's arm sent my mind spiraling back into distraction. *I was just supposed to volunteer today, not be captivated by a man.*

After we put everything away, he settled onto a nearby stool and asked, "So, what else do you like to do besides volunteer?"

A pleasant heat flared through my chest. "When I'm not working or worrying about my friend, I enjoy reading, road-tripping, the outdoors, and I've just begun going to church."

His eyes gleamed. "Sounds like we have a lot in common. What do you do for work?"

I held my head high. "I counsel kids."

Gabriel placed his hand over his heart and bowed. "You're an Earth Angel."

"Aw, thank you." I inched closer to him.

Pete walked toward us, clapping his hands. "Well, looks like you two got the bikes fixed. They're going to three sisters, and they'll be thrilled."

Gabriel gave a knowing grin. "Thank you for granting wishes, Pete. This was fun."

My thoughts had already drifted. Lou would've loved helping kids in this way.

Pete gestured for us to go to the front of the store. "Thanks for your help today. Hope to see you again." He opened the door, and we stepped outside into the sunlight.

Gabriel tucked his hands into his pockets. "Well, it was nice to meet you, Evie."

"You too. Thank you for helping me today," I said, eager to get home.

As I turned to leave, Gabriel tugged my arm. "Wait. Would you like to go out sometime?"

A glimmer of hope surfaced, and my pulse quickened. "I'd like that."

4

LOU

Sunlight streamed through the window, catching dust as it drifted in the air and settled on the coffee table. Saturday morning arrived, and Evie was coming over for garage sale shopping. The living room had items that brought me joy, like photos of Evie and my family, their smiles frozen in time. My gaze landed on my old address book, a bittersweet reminder of those who had once filled my life.

This house had been my constant—a silent witness to me as a carefree child, a hopeful young single woman, and now, a senior with cancer. The walls held echoes of laughter and conversations.

On the patio, the weathered swing teetered in

the wind. I went outside and lowered myself onto it, letting the gentle sway soothe me.

When I heard Evie's car, I pushed myself up, went to the front door, and yelled, "Hi."

As she walked up to meet me, she said, "It's nice to see you. How are you feeling?"

"I'm glad you're here. Come in." I led Evie through the familiar entryway and handed her a bag. "This is for the kids at school. It's full of toys and goodies."

"You're so kind. I'm sure they'll love them."

After locking the door, I looped my arm through hers, gripping my cane with the other hand as we hobbled to her car. Evie, ever patient, helped me in, then walked around to the driver's side.

"So, where are we going today?" My toes tapped in eager rhythm.

"A few sales around here." She started the car. "Then we can grab lunch. I've got a place in mind, but it's a surprise." While she drove down the street, she said, "We're overdue for a good laugh. Tell me that story again—the one from winter, with the letter."

"Oh, yes." The memory was still vivid. "It was icy that day, and I needed to mail something. I drove to the blue mailbox down the street, but I didn't want to fall, so I called out to an electrician working on a nearby house."

"That's right. What did you say?" Evie asked, beaming.

"I yelled, 'You-hoo! Can you please put my letter into the mailbox for me?'" I burst into laughter, hardly able to speak as I pictured the scene once again. "The man...took my letter, but instead of sliding it...into the public mailbox, he dropped it into the...mail slot of the...home he was working on by mistake."

We laughed so hard that we wept with joy.

Through giggles, she said, "That's such a funny story. Whatever happened to your letter?"

"I called the owners, and they slipped it into the mailbox on the street. Strange things seem to happen to me." I took a deep breath and added, "It feels so good to laugh after these past few days."

We arrived at the first sale and walked up the driveway. Treasures covered the tables. Evie sifted through puzzles, Rubik's Cubes, and fidget spinners for her students, while I picked out candles and kitchen gadgets for my neighbors.

Back in the car, I asked, "Did you get a good deal?"

"Sure did! What about you?" Evie put the key into the ignition and sped off.

"I got all my stuff for under five dollars!" I danced in my seat.

The other sales were similar—a mix of bargains and surprises. Evie spotted a purple scarf she adored. While she wasn't looking, I bought it for her, tucking it into my pocketbook.

Afterward, we stopped at my favorite pizzeria. The aroma of fresh dough, basil, and tomato met us at the door. Live music with mandolins and guitars drifted through the room.

We sat at a cozy table by the window and ordered sodas and a pizza.

"How are you feeling? Was this too much today?" Evie handed me a napkin and silverware.

A weary sigh escaped my lips. "I'm tired, but being with you was lovely."

The server brought our meal, and I asked, "So, what's new?" I placed a slice of pizza onto my plate.

Evie paused and then said, "I have some news, but it feels so trivial to what's going on with you."

I reached across the table, lightly squeezing her hand. "I still have life in me, and I want to hear it.

Today has been such a great distraction from the dread I've been feeling."

Evie rolled the napkin between her fingers. "I met a guy a few days ago."

My hand slapped the table, unable to contain my happiness. "Finally, some good news! Tell me all about him."

A shy smile bloomed on her face. "His name is Gabriel, and we met while volunteering. He asked me out. We both love being outside, traveling, and, most importantly, he's a Christian, too."

"He sounds like a match. Is he cute?" I teased.

She blushed, giving away her answer. "He's good-looking, with dark brown hair and a nice smile. And he's tall, too."

My heart warmed that she had met someone. This couldn't have come at a better time. "So, when's the date?"

"Actually, we just talked on the phone, and we're getting together this evening for a walk." Her voice bubbled with excitement.

"I know hearing about me being sick is hard, but I want you to take advantage of this opportunity with Gabriel. You're a gem, and you deserve someone special," I said, searching my purse for money.

"Thanks, and lunch is on me." Evie set cash on the table, and then we headed to her car.

Once we were inside, I handed her the scarf. "This is for you."

Her eyes twinkled. "Oh, my. I love it. Thanks for always spoiling me." Evie paused. "What else would you like to do today? Should we hit more sales, or—"

"Let's get an ice cream cone, and I'll pay this time," I said, licking my lips, anticipating the treat.

As we drove to Mary's Ice Cream Shop, I smoothed my hair under my cap. Bright red strands floated to the floor. Then, I fell asleep.

My eyes blinked open at Evie's whisper. "Here we are."

I felt my cheeks flush. "Sorry, I didn't mean to doze off."

"I'm glad you got some rest." Evie pulled into the drive-thru.

I handed her cash. "I'm getting my usual."

"Two small vanilla cones with sprinkles, please," she ordered. Then she turned to me. "Let's sit in the car and talk while we eat."

After she paid, Evie gave me my cone, and I licked it, crunching into the sprinkles as the creamy dessert slid down my throat. "This is so good."

"I know. It's heavenly," she said as she parked.

"So, what do you wanna talk about?"

"God. Tell me again about your relationship with Him," Evie said, as ice cream dripped into her lap.

A knot tightened in my chest. "Well, I used to believe in God, growing up in a Jewish household and all, but I don't anymore, because He's never answered any of my prayers." When Evie didn't say anything, I added, "I wanted to get married and have children, but that didn't happen. Then I lost my job, my family, and friends, and now I'll be losing you. See what I mean? God was never with me."

Evie leaned over. "I know we differ in our beliefs, and we've had some of the same letdowns, but He put me in your path for a reason."

"We were meant to be friends, for sure." We were in the right place at the right time, but I kept that part to myself.

"Unless people experience something, they're less likely to believe. I've asked this before, but if God came to you, would you believe in Him?" Evie licked the ice cream that was still melting down the sides of her cone.

"I'm not sure." My response had been the same over the years.

Evie crumpled her napkin, her gaze distant. "When I die, I hope to go to Heaven."

I glanced at her, weighing my response. "As you know, some Jewish people believe there's an afterlife with a loving eternal light, but I don't. Why the sudden interest in this today?"

Evie was tearful. "I'm worried that if you die, we won't be connected."

I frowned. "First, I'm not dead yet, and what do you mean?"

"Unless we both believe in God, our connection may fade." Sadness lingered in her eyes.

"I don't know what to say," I murmured, my thoughts spinning.

Evie's eyes held a spark of light. "I've heard that when we die, our loved ones are like angels and carry us to Heaven."

Her words pierced through me, and my heart swelled, pushing down the dread from our conversation. I reached for her hand and said, "You're my angel already. I don't know what I would've done without you."

5

EVIE

*A*fter I drove Lou home, I was eager to see Gabriel for our walk around Lake Immanuel. When I arrived, he was rocking in a chair on my porch with AirPods, wearing tan khaki shorts and a green shirt that made his olive skin glow.

He removed one earbud. "Hi, Evie. I was just listening to a meditation."

I nodded, excitement buzzing through me. "Thanks for meeting me here."

Mischief danced in his eyes. "Ready for our walk?"

"Almost. Just need to freshen up." I unlocked the door and invited him inside.

Sunlight poured through the bay windows,

lighting up my brown L-shaped couch, beige chairs, and a coffee table topped with a framed message about faith. Photos of rugged Colorado mountains decorated the walls, and the wooden floors gleamed.

Gabriel looked around. "This is nice."

I slipped off my shoes and sank into the familiar warmth of my home. "I moved in three months ago and still love it. Can I get you anything to drink?"

"Don't-a worry. I'm-a all set." He imitated an Italian accent.

I laughed. "You're good at that. Make yourself at home; I'll be right back."

In my bedroom mirror, I pulled my messy hair into a ponytail and added a touch of blush and gloss. When I returned to Gabriel, he was standing by the window, gazing into the wooded backyard.

Without turning, he said, "Some force calls me to nature. I could admire God's beauty all day. Do you hear the birds chirping?"

Two cardinals splashed in the birdbath, their red feathers catching the light. I grinned. "They come often."

He pointed. "Look, a squirrel is burying a nut in your yard—its safe haven. Trees give us oxygen. Everything has a purpose."

"How about we talk on our walk?" I nudged him toward the door. "I've been looking forward to this."

Outside, I asked, "Have you been to Lake Immanuel? Between moving and working, I haven't been out there yet."

"Yes, and it's close." Gabriel winked.

Butterflies fluttered in my stomach. The evening sun hid behind the clouds, and a cool breeze brushed my skin. Tall, century-old trees formed a green tunnel above us. The recent rain had turned the grass lush and vibrant.

I sighed with a sense of wonder. "Is the lake nice?"

He chuckled. "I don't want to spoil the surprise."

"When we talked on the phone, we didn't talk about work," I said.

He smiled faintly. "I retired from construction, and now I volunteer in hospice. Helping people who are dying is where my heart is."

I paused. "Why did you retire so young?"

He turned away. "I'd rather tell you another time."

Curiosity simmered, but I let it go. "How do you help people?"

"We talk, sometimes sit in silence. We listen to music, play games, or go outside."

"I couldn't do that. I'd be too sad." *If Lou were in hospice, that'd break me.*

When we reached the lake, I stopped, stunned. The crystal-clear water sparkled like diamonds. "Oh, my." I gasped in awe.

"Beautiful, isn't it? Take off your shoes. Come wade with me."

I did as he had asked, stepped onto the moist sand, and then walked with him into the water.

Calm ripples cooled our ankles. Colored rocks dotted the sandy floor, minnows darted like silver flashes, and snails crept along the ground.

"The water's so clear—like a magnifying glass. The critters almost reach for me."

Gabriel said, "Isn't it amazing? We all attract one another."

I admired his perspective—unlike anyone I'd met before. When his eyes locked onto mine, my heart pounded. Then I broke our gaze to focus on the entertainment in the water, my face warming as I felt Gabriel's stare.

After a few minutes, we went ashore, put on our shoes, and resumed our walk.

"I'd like to tell you a story. Something happened

recently that sums up why I love being with people who are dying. May I hold your hand?" Gabriel asked.

My heart skipped. "I'd like that." Our hands clasped, and a parade of goosebumps marched up my arm.

"The other day, I visited a dying patient who was unconscious. I prayed for him and asked God to lift him to Heaven," Gabriel shared, love radiating from his eyes.

Tingles coursed through me, sending electric pulses deep into my soul. "That was a beautiful prayer." I squeezed his hand.

Gabriel continued, "A man around our age came into the room and thanked me. He said I visited his dad when he couldn't. When he cried, I broke down, and we hugged. It wasn't one of those short, stiff man hugs, but it was a real one."

I stopped walking. "You remind me of a lightworker—someone who brings comfort and light."

"Caring for the sick and dying is what God wants." He nudged me. "Come, I want to show you something."

We stepped off the path, twigs crackling underfoot.

"Okay, we're here."

My breath hitched. There was a huge fairy garden with mini homes, mailboxes, trees, and lights. Cute animal figurines showed parts of Minnesota: Woodbeary, St. Paw, Snailing Avenue.

"Oh, I love fairy gardens! Why is it here?"

"That's a story for another time. It's getting dark. I want to learn about you. We'll come back." He pulled me to the trail.

His hand found mine again, anchoring me.

"So, I know the little you shared about your hobbies when we talked on the phone, but tell me more," he said with a bounce in his step.

I laughed. "What do you want to know? I'm an open book."

"Tell me about your family. Do they live close?"

The question caught me off guard. "It's a sad story."

"You don't have to tell me," he said gently.

I exhaled slowly. "I was put up for adoption as a toddler. I don't remember my birth parents. I went from one foster home to another, and it was rough. I never felt loved or wanted." Saying it out loud stirred an ache.

Gabriel turned and said, "I'm so sorry. I can't imagine what you went through."

A stray tear fell. "Thank you. My past is difficult to share, and I'll tell you more after we get to know each other better. What other questions do you have?"

"I just want to know all about you, so pick something and tell me." He slid his arm around me and continued our walk.

"I felt lost in high school, so a social worker helped me. Her name was Ms. Luz, and she accepted me and was always happy to see me. She made me want to help others. Now, I work in a middle school with kids."

When we reached the end of the path, Gabriel said, "That's inspirational. I'm glad you do what makes you happy, and thank goodness for Ms. Luz. Who supports you now?"

"Well, I tried finding my birth parents—dead end. Lou has cancer, so I might be alone again, but never without God. He's always been with me."

"I'm so sorry about your friend. It's heartbreaking when loved ones are sick." His eyes twinkled as if he saw something beyond.

6

LOU

*E*very limb ached. The pain was worsening and becoming more frequent. My new wig, purchased from the shopping channel last week, caught my eye. I slipped it on and peeked in the mirror. *Oh, no! It's burgundy instead of bright red, and it makes me look ancient.* Frustrated, I yanked it off and tossed it into the closet, where it joined my now-too-loose clothes.

After making my way downstairs, I collapsed into the armchair in the living room and drifted to sleep.

"Lou, wake up!" A familiar voice jolted me.

"Mom? Is that you?" I scanned the room, my heart pounding. "That was your…voice."

Something flickered in my peripheral vision. My

eyes darted toward the movement. Mom was in the mirror, her figure faint and transparent.

My stomach clenched, and my heart raced as I stood and hobbled closer to her, and then she vanished.

I shook my head. "That was a dream. It had to be. I don't believe in spirits." I sighed and sat on the couch, brushing off the eerie feeling that clung to my skin.

Evie will be here soon to take me to my doctor's appointment. These visits were always the same: a quick prick for blood and some polite questions about how I was feeling. My new normal.

I couldn't wait to hear about Evie's date. Afterward, I'd tell her all about me, except for my vision today. I didn't want her to think I'd believed what she'd said or, worse, convince myself I was nuts.

"Never mind," I muttered.

The doorbell rang, snapping me out of my thoughts. I'd forgotten to wait outside. I grabbed my cane and flung the door open.

"Hi, Evie." Her face glowed. *Must be the new man.*

"Ready to go?" she asked.

I grabbed a light jacket. "Let me lock up." Then I took her arm, and we walked to the car.

Once inside, Evie asked, "How do you feel about seeing your doctor?"

"I hate going to these appointments. I'd much rather be doing something fun with you." I toyed with the zipper on my coat.

"I know, but I'm glad I can take you. Maybe after, we can grab some ice cream or a bite to eat."

"Sure," I said, yawning.

A short while later, we pulled up to the one-story brick clinic. A chill ran across my neck at its cold, drab exterior. Evie parked and helped me out of the car.

Inside, the sharp scent of disinfectant hit me, unpleasant and sterile. I shuffled to the front desk to check in, then sank into a blue chair beside Evie.

She turned to me. "Do you want me to go into the room with you, or would you rather go alone?"

"Today's your lucky day. You get to come with me. And hey, you're my health care agent, remember?"

Three blue chairs, a small TV, and old photos of Lake Immanuel decorated the waiting area. A nurse called for the only other patient in the room, and then one came and called for me. She smiled and asked us to follow her.

When we got to the exam room, we sat down. The area was bare—an adjustable bed, a desk with a computer, and two extra chairs. *They really should make this place more inviting. Fluorescent lights are so harsh.*

"How are you feeling today?" the nurse asked.

I bit back what I wanted to say: *How do you think I'm feeling? I have cancer!* Instead, I said, "Achy and exhausted."

"Let's take your blood pressure and temperature. Then Dr. Grace will review the results of your scan."

I huffed. *Here we go.*

After a few minutes, the nurse frowned. "Your blood pressure is higher than last week, and you have a fever."

7

EVIE

*L*ou let out a weary sigh, her voice laced with frustration. "What now? More bad news?"

"Well, let's draw some blood and see what that shows," the nurse said, leading us to the lab.

Sweat coated my palms as my body tensed. *What if she's really, really sick? Worse than she let on? Will she die sooner than we thought?*

When we arrived, Lou sat in the chair while the nurse stepped out to gather supplies. She shifted uneasily. "I don't understand. I felt fine before coming here."

I reached for her hand. "Let's wait for the test results before we jump to conclusions." *Please God, let her be okay. We need a miracle.*

The nurse returned and instructed Lou to roll up her sleeve. "Okay, here's the prick."

I glanced away as the needle went into her arm.

"All done. Let's head back, and I'll get Dr. Grace," the nurse said.

Once the door to our exam room clicked shut, I said, "We'll hear what the doctor has to say, and then we'll make a plan."

Lou's face tightened with worry.

We jumped at a tap on the door. A slender, tall woman with wavy black hair stepped inside.

"Good morning, Lou." She offered a warm but professional smile. "And you must be Evie. I'm Dr. Grace."

"Hi." I bit my lip in anticipation.

Dr. Grace flipped through her clipboard. "I hear you're not feeling well—"

"I was feeling just fine," Lou snapped.

Dr. Grace's expression softened. "I understand. I've reviewed your scan from last week along with the results of your blood work."

She logged into the computer, pulling up an image on the monitor. "These are your lungs," she began, pointing to the screen. "This grayish matter is cancer, and as you can see, it's spreading to other parts of your body. This explains the elevated blood pressure and fever. We need to discuss next steps. You can either get care at home or move to Mercy Care Facility, where they have hospice. I'm so sorry this is happening." Her voice was gentle, her eyes filled with compassion.

My vision narrowed, and my chest squeezed. I felt faint.

Lou blinked, her voice barely above a whisper. "Hospice?"

Dr. Grace reached out, giving her arm a comforting squeeze. "Yes. I can't predict how much time you have left—it could be weeks, maybe months. We'll just have to see. I'm truly sorry. I know this is difficult to hear."

Weeks? This is happening too fast. My heart pounded while a tremble ran through my arms.

Lou rocked back and forth in her chair, her voice hollow. "Mercy is the only option for me."

Dr. Grace nodded. "I'll call to check if they have availability. I'll be right back." She stepped out, leaving us alone.

I stared at the monitor and said, "I think we need a second opinion. They should recheck the scan and run more tests to be sure."

Lou shook her head, her face pale and drawn.

"No, Dr. Grace is one of the best oncologists. I just wasn't expecting this today."

My heart shattered. "But I don't want to lose you. What if the tests are wrong?"

Tears streamed down Lou's cheeks. "Evie, this is hard for me too, but I trust Dr. Grace."

I bit back the rising lump in my throat. I didn't want to believe that she—we—were giving up, but she was the one who was sick. It was her decision. The thought of losing her so soon crushed me. It was a weight I couldn't bear.

A tap on the door pulled me from my thoughts.

Dr. Grace walked in. "Mercy has a room for you. Hospice will meet you there. You're familiar with it because of your sister, correct?"

Lou nodded, her gaze glued to the floor.

I managed to find my voice. "Why is this happening so quickly?"

"The cancer has been present for at least a year," Dr. Grace said. "Likely longer. Sometimes it spreads aggressively, like it is now. I'm so sorry."

I cried, "This is so sad."

"I didn't expect this news today," Lou said flatly.

As my lips trembled, I asked, "Can she sleep at home tonight?"

"Yes, but she needs to go to Mercy tomorrow

morning. They can't hold the room longer than a day."

We agreed and left the clinic in silence.

Once inside the car, I reached for Lou's hand, gripping it. "I thought we had more time."

Her voice broke. "Me too."

8

LOU

My heart shattered. Like everything else in my life, I was about to lose Evie. *How can God exist when all He creates is pain?* My fists clenched.

Evie wanted to stay with me, but I couldn't bear to have her see me like this. In the living room, my emotions erupted.

"Why is this happening to me?" I yelled, my voice cracking under the weight of despair. I collapsed onto the couch as sobs racked my body. *What will become of this place and all my treasures? And Evie?*

Regret burned in my chest. *I should've stayed here instead of moving into Mercy.* My heart ached as exhaustion settled deep into my bones. I was dying —there was no denying it now.

A flash of anger surged inside me. I grabbed the compass-shaped paperweight from the table and hurled it at the floor. Its shatter echoed across the room, cutting into the silence. I stared at the broken pieces.

Mom had given me that so I wouldn't lose my way. I'd planned to give it to Evie because, without me, how would she find her way?

My eyes focused on the dark, empty TV screen. The black abyss stared back, and I let out a guttural wail.

"There now, don't worry, Lou. We'll see you soon." Mom's voice, soft and familiar, drifted through the air like a comforting breeze.

My head shot up, my stomach knotting with confusion and fear. "Am I losing it, or am I already dead?" I whispered. When I looked at the mirror, it was clear.

Shaking, I reached for the phone. The line rang endlessly, and just as I was about to give up, Evie answered.

"Hello? Lou? Are you okay?"

I choked back a sob. "Yes, but I'm beside myself."

Evie's voice wavered. "I'm devastated, too. Do you want to talk, or should I come back over?"

"I don't want to talk about cancer anymore, but I'd love to hear about your time with Gabriel. We didn't get a chance to talk about that."

Her tone lightened, a small spark of warmth breaking through. "I'd love to tell you all about it."

As Evie recounted her date with Gabriel, her voice animated and full of life, I zeroed in on her words. For a brief, precious moment, our conversation lifted the sheer terror of imagining my last breath.

9

EVIE

*a*fter our call, heaviness settled in my chest. *God, please help Lou.*

The phone rang, and I answered it. "Hello?"

"Hi, it's Gabriel. How are you doing?" His cheerful voice made my stomach flip.

My head dropped into my hands. "Well, actually, I—"

Gabriel's mood shifted. "You okay?"

"No." I swallowed hard, steadying my voice. "I have some sad news."

"Is it about your friend?"

I sniffled, my breath hitching. "Ye…yes."

"Would you like me to come over?"

"I'd like that," I whispered.

After the call, I dragged myself into the shower.

The hot steam soothed my skin, but my heart still ached. *Lou can't die. Not now. Not ever.*

After I got dressed, the buzzer chimed, startling me. My heart raced as I ran to open the door.

Gabriel approached me with open arms.

"Hi," I said, sinking into his embrace. For a few minutes, the world's chaos faded. Though I hadn't known him for long, he made me feel safe. His calm demeanor created a protective bubble that shielded me from the storm raging inside.

A while later, I stepped away, wiping my eyes. "I'll be right back."

I struggled to regain my composure, retreated to the bathroom, and sat on the toilet. My thoughts swirled in a relentless cycle. *This isn't fair. I'm not ready to lose Lou, and what if she doesn't believe in God? Will we stay connected somehow? Please, God, give me the strength to face this.*

Gabriel tapped on the door. "Are you okay?"

"I...um...ahem. Yes, I'll be out soon."

"I ordered a pizza; it'll be here any minute. I'm starving. Have you eaten yet?"

My stomach growled. "No, but I should."

The doorbell rang. "I'll get it," he said.

I splashed water on my face, easing the knot in my chest, and then met him in the kitchen. I grabbed two bottles of water, plates, silverware, and napkins.

We moved the table and chairs to sit by the window where the moonlight spilled into the room. Its majestic glow offered comfort, like my Creator shining light into my darkness. I didn't want Lou to suffer, and yet I couldn't escape the dread gnawing at me.

Gabriel dished us a couple of slices of pizza and sat across from me.

I fidgeted with the food. "I'm glad you're here. It's hard being alone during a time like this."

Gabriel's eyes beckoned me to continue.

"Today was a whirlwind. At Lou's doctor's appointment, we learned the cancer had progressed. She'll be admitted to a care facility tomorrow and receive hospice." Tears rolled down my cheeks.

Gabriel reached across the table and rubbed my arm. "I'm so sorry. It's tough when this happens to someone we love."

I glanced at him. "Is there anything I should be doing to help her?"

"You can show her you're sad she's going through this. Try to remember, this is happening to her. She's the one with cancer, and her life is changing. You're important to her, so she's probably worried about you."

I took a deep breath, absorbing his words.

"Ask what she needs, but just visiting and talking helps more than you know. Try to keep things normal. Your friendship still matters, even now." He paused. "God calls us Home when we're ready. Lou's time is near, and she'll be okay."

I didn't know why he sounded so confident, but sorrow, like an anchor, weighed on my heart.

Gabriel's eyes mellowed. "Lean on me. Let me help you, but don't forget to get plenty of sleep and eat well. It'll help you through this. What care facility is she going to?"

I blinked, tears blurring my vision. "Mercy."

He nodded. "I know it well."

───────

The next day, a dark cloud shadowed my thoughts. As I drove to pick up Lou and take her to Mercy Care Facility, I wept. This would likely be the last time I'd see her at her house.

The Christian radio station played songs about letting go of things we can't control and living in the moment. A wave of gratitude washed over me, and I couldn't wait to see Lou.

When I arrived, she wasn't on the swing. I knew I'd miss seeing her there. As I walked up the sidewalk, I imprinted this final visit in my memory. At the top step, I rang the bell.

"Hang on!" Lou said, sounding unusually lively.

Then the door swung open, and she greeted me with a broad smile. "Hi! Come in."

I hugged her and trudged inside. "How are you?"

"I'm all packed, and I have something for you." She gave me a playful wink.

My vision clouded with tears. "I hope you didn't get me anything. All I want is to spend time with you." Lou picked up a shoebox from the floor and handed it to me. "I've collected a few things around here that I want you to have." Then, with a solemn expression, she gave me a crumpled piece of paper. "Hold onto this. When I get settled at Mercy, we'll go over it together."

I stuffed it into my pocket, blinking back tears.

Her hand rested on my arm. "No more crying. Dying is the next step in my journey—a chapter I'm ready to face. I've lived a long life, and right now, I want to spend time with my favorite person."

She nodded toward the stairs. "Could you do me a favor and bring my suitcase down? I just don't have the energy for it."

"Absolutely." A couple of minutes later, I lifted her luggage and called, "What do you have in this thing? It's so heavy!"

She laughed, the sound light and carefree. "Well, *you* try packing your whole life into one measly suitcase."

I smiled, carrying it down the stairs.

"Thank you. Let's do one last walk-through," Lou said, her shoulders sagging as she grabbed her cane and wobbled toward the kitchen.

Once there, I marveled, "Look at all of the sweets on the counter."

"I know. Tons. I'm going to miss choosing what I want to eat." Lou clutched her cane, knuckles turning white.

From there, we wandered into the dining room. The curtains and walls were dull, a sign that Lou was fading.

"When I was a kid, my family gathered here for meals, laughing and sharing stories. I'm going to miss this place."

"I'll miss seeing you here," I said, my voice catching in my throat.

Lou walked over to the mantle and stared into the mirror above it, as though she was expecting something to happen.

"Is everything okay?" I asked, curious about the sudden energy shift.

Lou waved her hand in the air as if to dismiss a thought. "I'm done now. Let's go before I start crying."

She locked the door as I maneuvered her suitcase and shoebox out to the car. When we looked at her house one last time, my eyes misted. "This was my home too, and I'll miss it," I whispered.

As we pulled into Mercy Care Facility, my gaze landed on the two Grecian pillars with cascading white flowers flanking the massive front doors. Several rooms boasted decks overlooking the shimmering Mississippi River.

After we parked, I said, "I'll get your suitcase."

"Thank you, dear." Lou opened her door.

I retrieved her luggage from the trunk and wheeled it to her. With my help, she eased out of the car and steadied herself with her cane.

Dragging her suitcase with one hand, I used the other to guide her to the front door.

Once inside, the brick walls created a warm and elegant atmosphere. Tall wooden beams stood throughout the lobby.

Lou checked in at the front desk. Then we rode the elevator to the third floor. When we got to room thirty-three, Lou used the keycard, and with suitcase in tow, we ambled in.

My eyes danced around the room—a leather couch, two chairs, and a small dining room, complete with a kitchen featuring stainless steel appliances, occupied the space. "Wow, this is lovely and…looks expensive."

"I know. I saved my parents' inheritance in a stock and cashed it out to pay for this place." Lou gestured to another doorway. "Come look at the bedroom."

It was breathtaking. An enormous window overlooked the river, paralleling the king-sized bed.

Lou walked across the living room. "Look at this deck." She slid the door open and hobbled outside.

The rush of the river greeted us as the sun graced my forehead like a quiet blessing. I wished time would stop.

Back inside, Lou asked, "Are you hungry? It's past lunch."

My stomach rumbled. "Is there a restaurant here?"

"Yes, but I feel like I ran a marathon today. Would you mind getting us something to eat?" She eased herself onto the sofa, her movements slow and deliberate.

"Sure." I wanted to see more of this place.

"Ask the woman at the front desk for directions, and please put it on my tab. I have an allowance, and I need to use it or lose it. Just give my name and room number."

I kissed her on the cheek and left. The hall was clean, with muted beige colors and soft lighting. I took the stairs down to the lobby.

At the front desk, an older woman greeted me with a smile. "How can I help you, dear?"

Her voice reminded me of when I met Lou. *If only we could go back in time, we would've had years together.*

I blinked out of the memory and asked, "Can you tell me where the restaurant is?"

"Of course, it's down that hall," she said, pointing. "We serve all meals there, but we also offer room service if needed. You're here with Lou Ireas, right?"

I hadn't heard her last name in a long time. I nodded. "How do you know?"

"I gave her the tour a few weeks ago. She's unforgettable—had me laughing the whole time with her funny stories."

I chuckled, imagining Lou in action. "I bet you've never met anyone like her."

She giggled, and then her expression turned serious. "Hospice is supposed to stop by soon to explain everything. You might want to get back so you don't miss them."

"Okay, thanks for your help." I hurried toward the smell of food.

Along the way, I saw a pool, a hot tub, and a community room where people were playing Bingo. Across the hall, folks sat watching a movie on a large screen. I made it to the restaurant and bought food, bottles of water, and her favorite—a pack of Chuckles.

When I returned to her room, I walked in and chatter filled the air. *Hospice must be here.* I put the food and drinks into the kitchen and announced, "I'm back."

"Good, dear, come here," Lou said.

I went into the living room, saw Gabriel, and froze.

LOU

*E*vie blinked, eyes wide with surprise. "Gabriel?"

"Hi." A smile spread across his face.

She glanced at me, then back at him. "What are *you* doing *here*?"

"This is where I visit my patients, and Lou's my newest one."

Evie stared at me. "Really? *You're* his patient?"

I gave a silent signal. '*Yes, isn't it marvelous?*'

Evie's cheeks flushed pink. "I didn't expect to see you here, but I'm glad you two met, and you're going to help Lou."

"Are you ready to talk about what happens next?" Gabriel's gaze settled on me.

When I nodded, he said, "Hospice is all about making sure you're comfortable."

"I'm so glad to have Evie, and now you, in my corner. She and I've been friends for a long time, and she's a godsend."

"May I ask about your religious preferences?" Gabriel retrieved a small notebook and a pen from his pocket.

My hand flew to my chest. "I can't believe I said that. I'm not religious or spiritual."

"Maybe we can talk about it another time." He paused, then said, "As you know, cancer may soon take over your body. You may lose the strength to eat and get out of bed. Significant pain is also possible, but we'll manage that for you."

My breathing slowed. "I don't want any life-prolonging meds. When it's my time, I want to go as naturally as possible."

Gabriel exuded warmth as he scribbled a note. He discussed important documents to ensure nothing had changed. We talked a bit about our lives, and then he stood and said, "Okay. I know food is waiting, and you must eat."

Evie was mesmerized by him.

He winked at her on his way out and said, "I'll see you both later."

After the door closed, Evie said, "I'm still in shock. He's on *your* hospice team?"

"Seems that way." This experience had deepened my connection with Evie and forged a new one with Gabriel. Perhaps I'd already uncovered moments of light.

Evie stood and walked into the kitchen, returning with plates, napkins, and food.

"I see you found the restaurant." I sat at the dining room table.

A grin tugged at her lips. "Yes, and I gave myself a little tour. It's nice here."

"I'm in good hands, and now I have a cute guy taking care of me, too." I laughed.

"Hey, he's off limits," Evie said, a smile playing on her lips as she joined me at the table.

"I know, I'm joking. What food did you get?"

"A sandwich and a couple of salads to share. You can eat what you want, but I'm starving." She handed me a bottle of water, then nudged the food toward me.

"Thanks. I'm not hungry anymore." I wrinkled my nose.

Evie's eyes shimmered. "What do you think about this place?"

Pain flared in my body. "I already miss my home, my privacy, and independence."

"I know, but I think you'll like it here, and I'll still visit you every day."

"Thank you, Evie." Tears pricked my eyes. "Having you here makes me feel ten times better."

EVIE

*J*hummed as I cleared the table, then joined Lou on the couch, hiding my hands behind my back.

"I have a surprise," I said, revealing a pack of Chuckles.

Lou lit up. "My favorite!" She eagerly opened the package and offered me one.

I picked spearmint while she chose her beloved black licorice.

"Before you go, can we talk about the paper I gave you?"

"Of course." I handed it to her.

She waved the note in the air. "This explains the five gifts inside the shoebox in your car. Open them in order."

Lou slipped on her glasses. "The first gift is a paperweight with twelve pennies suspended inside. I think the kids will love it. The morning before you came to Crossroads, I found a penny, heads up. I took it as a sign." She paused and rubbed her eyes. "The letters are moving. Maybe it's these glasses." Lou waved them in the air dismissively. "They were just a buck at the dollar store."

"I can read it for you," I offered.

"No, it's fine. The next gift is your favorite color —blue."

"I'll keep it close," I whispered, wiping away a tear.

Lou stared at the paper again, frustration flickering across her face. "The words are fuzzy, and I can't remember what I wrote."

"It's okay," I said gently.

Lou's lips curled into a mischievous grin. "Let's skip the rest. You'll find out soon enough. But the last gift matters most—and you'll love it."

I hugged her tightly. "Is there anything else I can do before I go?"

"I'm so tired. Can you help me to bed?"

I nodded. Once Lou stood, I draped my arm around her shoulders, and we walked to her room.

After she eased into bed, I pulled the covers over her.

"Thank you for being here. I love you," she murmured as her eyes closed.

"I love you, too." I prayed. *Please, God, watch over Lou when I'm gone.*

I finally left, heavy-hearted. In the elevator, I rolled my shoulders, hoping to ease the strain.

When I walked outside, it was late afternoon, and soft hues painted the sky. As I reached the car, a voice startled me.

"Fancy seeing you here."

My heart skipped, and I turned around. "Oh—hey, Gabriel."

"How's Lou?"

"She's sleeping. It's been a long day." I recalled the weariness on Lou's face as I helped her to bed.

"She needs rest." He paused. "I was just about to take a walk. Want to join me?"

"Can we meet at Lake Immanuel? I'd love to see the fairy garden again."

"I'll see you there," he said warmly.

On the drive to the lake, I couldn't stop thinking about Lou, and I felt bad for leaving her while I went out with Gabriel. Then I remembered what he told me, that it's good to take care of myself during this tough time.

As I rounded the corner to the lake, sparks ignited.

I saw his car, parked, and walked toward him.

"Hi," I said, smiling.

He hesitated as a nervous twitch crossed his brow. "May I hold your hand again?"

"I'd like that." A rush of euphoria fizzed through me as our fingers intertwined.

"Is it a conflict of interest for you to be on Lou's team?" I asked.

"No," he replied. "I'm a volunteer—I feel called to help her."

I exhaled in relief. "I know she tries to hide her pain, but I can still see it."

Gabriel nodded. "It's tough, but now she'll get the care she needs." He led me toward the garden where nature embraced us—trees bent protectively, and the ground softened.

I hesitated and then said, "Tell me more about the fairy houses."

"No one knows who put them here." He winked at me. "But one day, the fairies moved in."

"They grant wishes, too, right?" I teased.

"Yep. Fairies are light beings that come to uplift."

Hope flickered inside me.

"Here we are," he said.

Before us lay a magical village: tiny wells, trees, benches, and bridges all blended with nature. Colorful statues of fairies—children, elders, and pets—peppered the space. At the center of it all stood a glowing cross, radiant and otherworldly.

"This is incredible," I breathed.

Gabriel pulled out pens and paper and handed them to me. "Write some wishes. We can put them in the houses, but don't tell me what they are."

I sat on a tree stump and leaned in to write. My first wish was for Lou: to be met with light when she passed, and for peace in her absence. Second, that we'd stay connected, and third, that my bond with Gabriel would grow. When I finished, I handed the notes to him.

"Oh no," he said. "You place them. The fairies believe energy travels from your hands."

I slipped my first wish into a blue, three-story fairy house. Then I found a tiny church, brimming with wishes. It felt sacred, perfect for my deepest desire to stay connected with Lou. I knew this holy shrine would anchor my wish, so I slid it inside. For Gabriel, I chose a brown-and-red, shoe-shaped home. The white laces were symbolic, while the shoe itself evoked the miles we might walk together. Inside, a tiny cross glowed. A soft breeze brushed my neck, like an unseen blessing.

Our eyes fused, and Gabriel asked, "How do you feel?"

"Better. God hears us—I know He's with us in this special sanctuary."

I turned to leave, but Gabriel caught my arm, his touch warm and grounding. "Wait."

When I pivoted toward the fairy village, it burst into light, glowing with a radiance that pulsed and shimmered with energy.

"Fairies are spiritual creatures," he whispered.

Another breeze caressed my neck, and this time, hundreds of fireflies suddenly filled the air, glittering like stars.

"Wow," I gasped, tingling with delight.

Then, his voice low and reverent, Gabriel said, "I'd like to kiss you."

I nodded as my heart thudded, each beat filling me with a rush of anticipation.

Gabriel lifted my chin, and our eyes locked. Then his lips, soft and perfect, found mine as the world dissolved around us.

LOU

I tossed and turned all night, clinging to the hope that hospice was just a bad dream, but every time I awoke, reality hit me. The sharp scent of disinfectant lingered in the air, anchoring me to the present.

A deep, dull pain throbbed throughout my body, rendering me immobile. Still, I needed to use the bathroom, so I buzzed for a nurse.

Moments later, there was a tap on the door. "Lou, do you need something?" a young, gentle voice called.

"Yes. Help getting to the bathroom." I grimaced.

The nurse walked over to me, her white scrubs pristine, her long red hair flowing down her back.

She radiated a loving glow, her piercing green eyes touching my soul.

"I'm sorry to bother you. I'm sure you have other patients, but I'm in so much pain, and I don't have the energy to get out of bed. It's like my body just...stopped working."

"Don't worry, dear," she said, smiling. "I'm Iris, and I'm here to help. There's nothing to be embarrassed about. Sometimes our bodies go into shock and refuse to cooperate."

Her name reminded me of my last name. As she lifted the blanket and helped me sit on the edge of the bed, a wave of calm washed over me.

"All right," Iris said gently. "Can you move your legs? Maybe they're just stiff."

I flexed my muscles, hoping I wouldn't wet myself in the process.

She disappeared briefly before returning with a walker. "We're going to manage just fine."

Her confidence was contagious, and I summoned the strength to push myself up, gripping the bed rail and reaching for the walker. I puffed my chest in victory, though my body burned with fatigue.

Iris smiled and tucked a stray lock of hair behind her ear.

"You're beautiful," I blurted.

"We are, aren't we?" she said, her gaze steady and knowing.

I wasn't sure what she meant, but the urgency in my bladder made any lingering questions irrelevant.

With Iris coaching me, I leaned on the walker and shuffled toward the bathroom. When we reached it, she closed the door behind me.

I heaved a sigh of relief, grateful to see the toilet.

As I washed my hands, water flowed in slow motion. Droplets swirled between my fingers like tiny galaxies. A strange, profound peace washed over me, and I stood captivated.

Afterward, when I opened the door, Iris' eyes sparkled. "See? I knew you could do it! You're stronger than you think."

I limped back to bed, every step more difficult than the last. "I feel like a bus hit me." I collapsed onto the mattress.

"When we're sick, our bodies work overtime to keep up," she explained, propping my pillows and tucking the sheets around me. Her face lit up. "Don't worry, it's wonderful on the Other Side."

"Is it?" I whispered, unsure I wanted to hear the answer.

"Look!" she said, pointing at the window. "It's going to be a sunny day."

I followed her gaze to the horizon, where the sun peeked through the clouds in golden rays.

"I'm glad I have a window seat," I murmured.

When I turned back to Iris, my breath caught in my throat.

She was gone, and all that remained was the walker.

"Iris?" I called out, but the room was dead silent. "Where did she go?" I mumbled.

"Who're you talkin' to?" Gabriel startled me as he sauntered into the bedroom.

A soft thrill brushed over me at hearing his voice.

"Is it okay that I'm here?" he asked.

"Of course. Any friend of Evie's is a friend of mine."

He sat beside my bed. "So, who were you talking to?"

"Iris. One of the nurses. She helped me to the bathroom, then disappeared without saying goodbye." I glanced around, expecting her to reappear.

"Hmm, I don't know anyone by that name. It could be a new hire or—"

"Yes?" I asked, intrigued.

Gabriel leaned closer and said, "Or she could've been a vision. An angel, perhaps."

I raised an eyebrow, stifling a laugh. "You sound just like Evie, and I'm not religious."

He chuckled. "Angels aren't about religion. I think we all have guardian angels, whether we believe or not. They love us unconditionally."

I thought about seeing Mom back home.

Gabriel's voice dropped into an almost otherworldly tone. "When people are dying, their senses sometimes reboot. It's like restarting a computer. Our senses heighten, and we tune into things others don't notice. I think what you saw was an angel. Life slows down in these moments, and we become deeply connected—to everything."

Maybe Iris was an angel. I thought about it and shook my head. "Some people believe in that stuff, but I don't."

"That's okay," Gabriel said kindly. "Can I tell you a story?"

I nodded, welcoming a distraction, even though pain radiated up my spine.

Gabriel turned toward the window. "Once, I knew someone who didn't believe in God. He thought nothing divine had a place in his life, but then one day, when he went to work, there was an accident, and he died."

I gasped. "Oh no, I'm so sorry."

"That's one of the risks of being a construction worker." He hesitated. "If we could keep this between us for now, I'd appreciate it."

"It's our little secret." I winked, hoping to lift the mood.

Then an ethereal glow pulsed out from his body, and Gabriel said, "I'd like to tell you what happened after he passed. Is it okay if I stay a little longer?"

As I focused on the soothing light, my pain lessened, but when I blinked, the sight disappeared, and the pain returned, stronger than before.

I frowned. "Did you see that bright light?"

"No," he said, tilting his head.

"That's strange," I murmured.

Gabriel marveled, "So, after he died, a miracle unfolded."

"Oh?" I shifted, eager to hear more.

"I had a vision. My friend came face-to-face with Jesus. And guess what?"

I shrugged, unable to imagine.

"Jesus embraced him, and a pure, radiant light surrounded us. It wasn't just bright—it was love itself. Vibrant colors, more beautiful than anything on earth, swirled around us." Gabriel showed me the scene with his hands. "And the best part, do you know what that was?"

"No." I shook my head, bracing for his answer.

"Jesus said, *'I've loved you since before you were born, and My love for you is infinite.'*" Gabriel's voice trembled with emotion. "He forgave us, and we felt His divine love. It was transformative."

Tears spilled down my cheeks. *The Almighty comes for everyone—except me.*

Gabriel turned to me and said, "Since then, my connection to God has been unshakable, and He gave me a gift—a sixth sense, if you will. I feel things others don't, and I communicate with the world in ways I never imagined. That's why I was called to hospice—to help people feel His presence."

Though my body was dying, my soul felt reborn. Then I remembered what Evie had said: "Unless people experience something, they're less likely to believe."

13

EVIE

J sat on the couch, sipping coffee while the sun bathed the living room, painting the walls with a soft morning light. My mind snapped into focus, and I wondered how Lou was doing.

Then I thought about the lovely kiss Gabriel had given me in the fairy garden. Heat spread through me, followed by quiet waves of bliss—until a sinking feeling settled in, tugging me like an anchor.

I paused and reached for the phone to dial Lou's room at Mercy.

"Hello?" Her voice, though strong, carried a faint undercurrent of strain.

"Lou, it's me, Evie. How are you today?" I hoped my unease was misplaced.

"Well, I've had a pretty eventful morning, but I'm not dead yet, so I'm good." She chuckled.

Her comment didn't make me laugh. "I should be there within twenty minutes. What can I bring? Are you hungry? Do you have any cravings?"

"No, I just want to spend time with you, and guess what? Gabriel's here, and we've been talking for a while."

My spirits lifted, easing the knot in my chest. "That's great. Please tell him hi for me, and I'll be there as soon as I can."

I spotted the shoebox sitting by the door, and a rush of sadness hit me like a wave.

I grabbed my sweater and a card, locked up, and drove to Mercy. I couldn't wait to see Lou.

When I arrived, I ran up to her room and pushed open the door.

"Hello?" I called, out of breath.

"We're in here," Lou replied.

I put the card in the kitchen and followed the familiar sound of voices.

Gabriel was next to Lou in her bedroom, and my heart leapt at the sight of him.

"Hi, you two," I said.

A faint blush warmed Lou's cheeks. "Glad to see you."

Gabriel stood. "I need to visit my other patients. I enjoyed our time together, Lou. And Evie, wonderful to see you again. You're glowing." His eyes gleamed with sincerity.

Tingly sensations glided down my neck. "Nice to see you too, and I'll see you later."

After he left, I took a seat near Lou. "How are you feeling?"

"I'm in a lot of pain, but it's manageable." Her voice was steady but tired. "My night was rough, and this morning was worse. I needed to use the bathroom, and the strangest thing happened."

Lou recounted her experience with the mysterious nurse who had vanished.

"Then what happened?" I asked, curious.

"Gabriel came for a visit. I told him about her, and he thought she was an angel," Lou said with a slight shrug.

"An angel?" I echoed, a gentle breeze tickling my arm. "Maybe she was sent from God."

Lou rolled her eyes in playful disbelief.

I laughed. "Hang on." I retrieved the card from the kitchen and handed it to her.

"What's this?" she asked, taking it.

"It's for you. I wrote it last night." I smiled.

"You're so thoughtful. Should I open it now?"

"If you'd like. And I'm sorry you didn't have a restful night—and that your morning was...well, interesting," I added.

Lou gave the card to me, her eyes twinkling. "Can you please read it to me? You know what happened the last time I used my glasses."

I grinned, taking the card back. Then, clearing my throat, I read: "Dear Lou: You've changed my life. I'll always remember your bright red hair and spirited self. I loved working alongside you all those years, helping children together. I'm so thankful for our garage sale adventures, our outings to eat, and of course, our many ice cream cones. I enjoyed hearing your stories and laughter, which encouraged me to laugh too." I wiped a tear.

Lou's face brightened. "Oh boy, we had fun, didn't we?"

My hand covered my heart in a sign of gratitude, and then I continued reading. "I adored our shared love for sweets, and I'll think of you every time I step into a candy store. We were in Heaven, yet still on Earth. Thank you for including me in your world. I've been seen and found, loved and cherished—things I never had. Just because we'll be in two different places doesn't mean I won't see you again. I'll always love you. Love, Evie."

14

LOU

*A*fter some much-needed laughter and catching up with Evie, exhaustion crept over me. She left with promises to visit again soon. As the quiet settled in, her heartfelt words replayed in my mind, and tears welled in my eyes.

Today had been a whirlwind: the angelic vision, the strange water phenomenon in the bathroom, Gabriel's radiant presence, his story, and my time with Evie, hearing how deeply I had impacted her. It was almost as if—dare I say—God was inviting me to believe.

There was a lot to consider, and not much time to do it. I vowed that tomorrow, I'd try to make sense of life, death, and God. I had always strived to do the right thing, but something vital was missing.

I drifted off into an uneasy sleep, waking only at lunchtime. A tray with soup and salad sat on the bedside table, but I wasn't hungry. My body demanded rest, so I surrendered to sleep once more.

I awoke after dinner, and the untouched food was gone, replaced with fresh water. I forced myself to the bathroom, where the mirror reflected a stranger. My face was pale, shadowed by dark circles, and my hair, once vibrant, now fell in wisps. I had aged.

Pain shot through my body as I crawled back into bed. Through the window, I stared at the endless night sky. Thousands of stars shimmered like they were drawing closer, their brightness wrapping around me, like a tender embrace. Comforted, I fell into a deep sleep.

When I woke, it felt like my body was on fire. It was five in the morning—three hours until breakfast.

Memories surfaced—Mom at home, the angelic presence, and Gabriel's story. Each moment seemed to point to something bigger. My eyes wandered to the wall, where a Star of David hung—a symbol that hadn't been there before.

God had always been with me. I now know He'd been waiting for me to see, to trust.

I reached over to the bedside table and opened the drawer, finding a small pen and notebook. My hands trembled as I confessed, "This is another sign You exist."

Tranquility enveloped me, and energy coursed through my weary muscles. With a heart both heavy and grateful, I began to write. Words flowed out effortlessly, a letter filled with everything I'd held inside.

As I finished, a voice echoed in my mind—deep, resounding, unmistakably kind.

"Lou, I've always loved you. Before you were born, until now, and for all eternity."

Tears streamed down my cheeks as I folded the letter and set it on the bedside table. I pulled the covers over me and closed my eyes. Peace embraced me, and I fell into the deepest sleep I'd ever known.

———

"Good afternoon, Lou! Rise and shine," a deep, familiar voice greeted me.

Had I died? The thought made me shiver. I turned my head to the sound, but my body resisted, stiff and unyielding. Squinting against the sunlight, I asked, "Where am I?"

"You're still at Mercy," Gabriel replied, his tone soothing. "You've slept a lot today."

I sighed, disoriented. "What time is it?"

"Three in the afternoon," he said, adjusting the blinds to soften the light.

"Oh my! I've never slept this long."

"That's a good thing." He helped me sit up.

"My spirit feels well-rested, but my body…it's in excruciating pain. My limbs ache, and I'm completely drained."

"Would you like any pain medication?" Gabriel asked, concern etched in his face.

I shook my head, wincing at the effort. "No, if I'm on my way out, I want to be present. I don't want to miss a moment, even like this."

Gabriel nodded.

"I had such an incredible day yesterday, and I have you to thank for helping awaken my faith. Your story—it opened a door I've kept closed for so long." A smile tugged at my lips. "I don't know if I'll have enough time to tell Evie what I've decided about God, but it's all here." I reached for the letter and handed it to him. "Could you make sure she gets this?"

His eyes dimmed as he took it. "Of course, and I know just the place to keep it safe."

Then, the phone rang, and Gabriel handed it to me.

"Hi, Lou!" Evie's voice burst through the line, a mixture of relief and worry. "I called earlier, but Gabriel said you were sleeping. How are you?"

"Well, I just woke up. It hurts to move, and I don't feel like myself."

Evie paused and then said, "Okay, I'm leaving right now. I love you."

"I love you, too. More than you'll ever know."

I handed the phone back to Gabriel and closed my eyes, surrendering to the stillness within. I felt myself being drawn inward to a quiet place deep in my soul.

15

EVIE

*M*y fingers trembled on the steering wheel as I sped to Mercy, my mind racing. The phone rang, and I answered it.

"Evie, this is Gabriel." The urgency beneath his voice tightened my chest. "I have a hunch Lou will be going Home today. I'd suggest you come quickly."

A knot coiled in my stomach. "I'm on my way," I said, my voice breaking. "But why so soon? Her doctor didn't say it was this close. I thought we had more time." Tears blurred the road ahead.

"Everyone's journey is different. She's declining faster than we'd hoped. My guess is her body is shutting down in ways we can't fully see."

I cried, "This is so hard."

"I know, and I'm sorry. I'll see you soon." Gabriel ended the call.

I gripped the steering wheel tighter, my knuckles white. *Oh no, God! Not today! It's too soon!*

My leg bounced as panic swirled inside. The drive became a haze of fragmented prayers and hurried breaths. By the time I parked, my mind was racing too fast to process the simple act of walking. I bolted to Lou's room, barely aware of the world around me.

Inside, Gabriel was seated at Lou's bedside, hunched forward, his hands clasped in silent prayer. He looked up as I entered, his eyes filled with compassion. "I'm glad you're here. She was in pain earlier, but said she felt rested. She didn't look well, fell asleep, and hasn't been responsive since."

His words landed like a physical blow. I swayed, my heart sinking to my stomach.

Gabriel stood, embraced me, and for a brief moment, the world slowed. "I'll give you some time alone with her."

After he left, the room felt suffocatingly quiet. My knees wobbled as I sank into the chair beside Lou's bed. The sight of her motionless form hit me harder than I expected. Tears cascaded down my face as I reached for her hand.

"Hi, Lou. It's Evie. I'm here now," I choked out, my voice trembling. "I've been praying for us to have more time together. I know that's selfish, but I'm not ready to say goodbye." I sniffled. "We had such a good time yesterday. I wanted to revisit the conversation about God. I don't know how you left it with Him, but I hope—" I paused, the lump in my throat growing. "I just don't want this to be goodbye forever. I love you so much, and I'll miss you."

For a second, silence answered.

Then, through labored breaths, Lou whispered, "I love you too, Evie. And don't worry."

My heart surged with gratitude, the sound of her voice a fleeting but cherished gift.

Then her breathing hitched, shallow and uneven. Her chest rose once more, then fell, never rising again. Her hand in mine went slack.

"Lou?" My voice cracked with desperation. I searched for any sign of life, pleading for just one more moment with her.

When she didn't respond, my heart squeezed, and a loud cry heaved, raw and unrestrained.

I stayed by her side for an hour, unable to move, the weight of her absence pressing down on me.

God, please take care of this lovely soul, I prayed silently, my tears an offering of love and loss.

———

When I got home, I went straight to bed, but the night offered no rest. I tossed and turned until six in the morning, and then I finally gave up, walked into the living room, and sank into the couch.

The shoebox remained on the floor, holding everything I'd lost. I picked up the list of items, wanting to see what was inside, desperate for a connection to Lou.

I lifted the box, carrying not just objects but memories. Then I brought it to the sofa, took off the lid, and unwrapped the items one by one.

The first was a clear, square penny-filled paperweight. At a closer glance, the pennies were heads up, like the one Lou found the day we met. My eyes misted.

Next, I found the gift Lou had cherished most: a smooth, swirling orb of blue hues that fit perfectly into my palm. As I held it, a tingle sparked my skin. I set it down, startled, but I picked it up again, and the sensation grew stronger. A mix of longing and joy overwhelmed me.

"Lou," I breathed. "I know you're here with me."

I opened the third gift, and a small angel clip fell out. My brow furrowed. I checked the list and read aloud: "Evie, we spent a lot of time in your car, so this is to ensure angels protect you while you drive." I turned it over and found an inscription: *Don't go too fast, so the angels can keep up.* Tears stung my eyes, but I smiled through them.

The fourth item was a framed photo of us at the candy store. The note read: "Evie, you've meant the world to me. I'll always remember you." On the back of the picture, there was a handwritten message: *To Evie, my forever friend and family. Love, Lou.*

The final gift chimed as I removed the tissue. Lou's bright red lanyard fell out with three keys, their rims glittering red, brown, and white—the same colors as the fairy shoe where I'd placed my wish about Gabriel. It couldn't be a coincidence. I read the note: "Evie, having keys that opened things comforted me. You never know—you might need one of these keys someday. Love, Lou." I pictured the lanyard draped around her neck, always so sure of herself, yet leaving me something to hold onto.

I lay on the couch, stacking her gifts on my stomach. The love Lou poured into these small, powerful tokens lulled me into a deep, peaceful sleep.

A soft chirp startled me awake, and I fumbled for my phone on the coffee table. It was a text from Gabriel: *Meet me at eight at Lake Immanuel. I'll see you soon.*

I sent a quick heart emoji in reply. *Why does he want to meet there?*

After eating breakfast, I got ready, locked the door, and hopped into my car. The memory of Lou's final moments flooded my mind, my stomach tightening with each mile.

I arrived, and the sun was bright, the sky a clear blue—perhaps another sign. I parked and spotted Gabriel waiting.

As I walked toward him, he came to meet me, arms open. I fell into his embrace with a tired sigh.

"Good morning, Evie. How are you feeling today?"

After we hugged, my voice trembled. "I'm so sad. Everything feels like a bad dream. I can't believe Lou isn't here anymore."

"It's heartbreaking," he said, holding my hand. "But I'm glad you were with her yesterday."

I squinted against the sunlight. "Why are we here so early?"

He offered a small but hopeful smile. "Let's visit the fairies," he suggested, gently guiding me forward.

We walked there in heavy silence, my eyes burning with tears.

Once we reached the garden, he stopped and asked, "Do you see anything different?"

I gasped, "Oh, my! The fairy chapel is glistening."

Drawn by wonder, I hurried over to it and dropped to my knees. As I opened its tiny doors, a rush of brilliant white light flowed out, momentarily blinding me. Blinking away the dazzle, I peered inside—and saw something waiting for me.

"There's a note with my name on it," I said, pulling it out.

Gabriel stepped closer, and his face lit up. "Look what you found—and in a church, of all places."

My hands shook as I unfolded the note. Heart racing, I read aloud: "Dear God - Recently, I've learned to believe and trust in You and welcome Your eternal light. Please take care of Evie, hold her close to Your heart, and watch over Gabriel, as he needs You too. Knowing You fills my heart with overflowing love and gratitude. I've seen Your light, heard Your loving words, and known You've always been with me. Thank you! Love, Lou."

I weeped. "Lou found God!" I turned to Gabriel, trembling with joy. "This is why she told me not to worry! I'm so happy she found Him!"

Gabriel twirled me around in celebration, and then his lips met mine in the softest, most tender kiss I'd ever experienced.

Afterward, I hugged him tightly. "Thank *you* for finding *me*," I whispered.

16

EVIE

After leaving the fairy garden, Gabriel had to return to his patients, but he suggested we meet tomorrow because he had something to tell me.

On my way home, I stopped for ice cream to celebrate Lou's newfound faith. As I savored my vanilla cone with sprinkles, I broke into a grin, remembering how Lou lit up during our final treat together.

It comforted me to know she had passed peacefully, believing in God. I was grateful that we had said we loved each other before her last breath. The road ahead would be difficult, but with Gabriel and God by my side, I wouldn't have to face it alone.

When I got home, I changed into my pajamas and lay in bed. The late morning sun filtered through the window, cradling me to sleep.

A loud ring startled me awake, and I reached for my phone.

"Hello?"

"Evie, it's Gabriel. Did I catch you at a bad time?"

I rubbed my eyes, still groggy. "I must've fallen asleep. What time is it?"

"It's nine in the morning," he said, a note of concern in his voice.

"Wow, I went to bed yesterday morning."

"It's been a tiring few days," he acknowledged.

A flutter stirred in my stomach. "Aren't we getting together today?"

"Yes, I was thinking we could have a picnic at our lake." His tone lifted with excitement.

"That sounds perfect! What time?"

"Could I pick you up around noon? Don't worry about food; I've got it covered."

"Okay, I can't wait." I hung up, a soft smile lingering. *I miss you, Lou, but I'm glad I won't be alone today.*

After I got dressed, the phone rang again. I

squinted at the unfamiliar number and then answered it.

"Hello? Is this Evie Celeste?" a woman asked, her voice polite.

"Yes, how can I help you?" I replied, puzzled.

"My name is Angelina, and I'm the head oncology nurse at Mercy." She hesitated before continuing. "First of all, I'm so sorry for your loss. Lou was such a kind soul."

"Thank you," I said, my voice breaking. "I miss her already."

"Well, before Lou moved in, she left us a locked box with instructions to give it to you after she passed. When would you be able to come pick it up?"

A locked box? Oh, Lou.

We agreed that I'd come right over.

My heart raced as I hurried out the door. I slid into my car and drove to Mercy, my mind buzzing with questions.

When I arrived, I rushed to the front desk and asked for Angelina. Moments later, a petite woman with jet-black bangs and piercing blue eyes approached.

"Hello, Evie. I'm Angelina. Let me grab the box for you. I'll be right back."

Bittersweet memories hit me as I stood in the quiet lobby. Now, Lou's absence felt even more real, but I'd never forget our final goodbye.

Angelina returned, and as she placed the box on the counter, she said kindly, "This is it. There's no key, but you can take it with you. It was nice to meet you."

"Thank you," I muttered, my heart pounding.

On my way home, I wondered if one of the keys on Lou's lanyard would open the box, and then my mind spun with thoughts about what she might have left behind.

When I arrived, I sat on the couch and pulled out the lanyard. One by one, I tried the keys, my hands trembling. The red-rimmed key slid in the lock and clicked, and my breath caught.

I gently opened the box and saw a yellow padded envelope. I unsealed it, and a business card slid out. It was from Lou's attorney, with a dollar sign scribbled next to the contact information. Perhaps she had left me money. My heart thudded in disbelief.

"Wow," I said, my voice shaky.

There was more: a note from Lou. Slowly, I unfolded it and began to read: "Evie, our friendship means so much to me. Thank you for loving me. I'll always love you, and I hope you'll find peace with my passing. Maybe we can still be connected, as you wished. I've transferred the house deed to you, and please use the money for whatever you need. Love, Lou."

I stared at the note, stunned, then re-read it a few times, slowly absorbing her gifts of friendship. I loved reading her words of adoration, excited by the possibility that we might reconnect, and I was in awe that she had left her home to me—what I thought I'd lost was now mine to keep.

17

EVIE

Gabriel picked me up for our picnic at the lake. As we drove, I shared my visit to Mercy and the incredible things Lou had left me.

"She was special, wasn't she?" he asked.

"Yes, and I'm so glad I had the opportunity to know her." Lou was the most thoughtful person I'd ever met.

"Have you felt her presence yet?" Gabriel glanced at me, his expression kind.

I hesitated, then nodded. "When I held the paperweight, there was this tingly sensation. It could be her." My heart swelled with hope.

"That's great." He smiled, turning into the parking lot.

We got out of the car, and Gabriel retrieved a picnic basket and two chairs from his trunk. Together, we found a private spot just steps from Lake Immanuel. The sunlight sparkled on the water's surface, and a gentle breeze carried the scent of fresh-cut grass.

Once we settled in our chairs, Gabriel said, "I made veggie sandwiches. We also have fruit, chips, and brownies for dessert. There are plates and napkins. Would you like a bottle of water?"

"Yes. Thanks for doing this." I was touched.

He handed me water and fixed a plate for me, then one for himself. We sat facing the lake, enjoying the rhythmic sound of waves lapping the shore.

Gabriel turned to me and spoke, his voice steady. "I'd like to share how I came to know Jesus."

"I'd love to hear your story," I replied, curious.

Gabriel's gaze shifted back to the lake. "I was a working-class man. Never married, no kids. Like you, I'm estranged from my family, but they're still alive. That's a story for another time. My parents didn't raise me to believe in God or Jesus, so I never went to church. The only person I cared about was myself." He sipped his water.

I blinked, surprised. "That doesn't sound like you at all."

"I know. I worked in construction, watched movies, surfed the web, and had the occasional drink. Then, one day, there was a tragic accident at work, and I died."

I gasped. "You died?" I pivoted my chair to face him, the weight of his words sinking in.

He nodded, meeting my eyes. "Yes, I don't remember the exact details, but there I was, lying in a hospital. As my soul levitated, I saw that the doctors were trying to save me. That's when I realized I was dead."

I leaned forward, struggling to process his words.

"There was a brilliant white light," he continued, his voice tinged with awe. "Then Jesus was standing right beside me. I was overjoyed. His love wrapped around me like a warm blanket. I asked for His forgiveness for not believing in Him, and as radiant colors swirled around us, He said, *'I've loved you since before you were born, and My love for you is infinite.'*"

Tears spilled down my cheeks.

"He told me I had a purpose on earth. At the time, I didn't fully understand Him. Then He revealed the unity of the Father, Son, and Holy Spirit."

Gabriel wiped a tear. "I now know that unity is what we call the Holy Trinity—three divine persons who are one. While I was resting and healing, God told me whoever was connected to multiples of three would walk with Him and heal others."

The Trinity necklace that Gabriel wore at the bike shop snapped into focus, but I didn't want to interrupt.

"God saved me from the emptiness of my old life," Gabriel admitted, his eyes glistening. "He told me I had a gift to share. Then, my soul returned to my body, and as the doctors performed CPR, my heartbeat resumed."

My chest expanded, a sense of wonder building within. "What was the gift?"

"God said He'd show me how to help and heal others." He wiped his tears.

I moved to embrace him, unable to contain my emotions. My heart overflowed with gratitude—for Gabriel and God's grace.

When we pulled apart, Gabriel sat back down, a soft smile on his lips. "The doctors were astounded. They called it a miracle."

I let out a long breath. "I'm so glad you're okay."

"So am I," he said. "God gave me a second chance. Now, I'm closer to Him than ever. I communicate with Him daily, and my work with hospice helps me understand my gift. By the way, I shared a simpler version of this story with Lou, one she could relate to."

My spirit soared. "I think your story helped Lou find God."

Gabriel's expression turned serious. "I believe Lou lived the life God intended for her. She was Jewish, but her living on Trinity Lane was no coincidence. On the day she died, she woke up at three. There's that number again. She was on the third floor at Mercy, and her room number was thirty-three. I don't know much about Judaism, but there's a Hebrew symbol, chai, which means life. It's associated with two numbers that add up to eighteen, a multiple of three. I wonder if the number three appeared in other ways for her."

I racked my brain. "Oh my! Three firefighters went to her house, and Lou's sister passed away three years ago."

Gabriel's mouth curved into a knowing smile.

"What about in your life? Where has that number shown itself?"

I reflected, and then it clicked. "I moved into my home three months ago. Lou and I were thirty years apart. She gave me a paperweight with twelve pennies, and her third gift was an angel clip. And, I stuffed my wish for her into a three-story fairy house."

"Speaking of that, have your wishes come true yet?" he asked.

"Yes, a couple of them. I suppose I can share them with you."

He gestured for me to continue.

"My first wish was that Lou would be met with loving eternal light when she went Home, and that she accepted God before she died. My next wish was for us to stay connected, and she's been with me."

Gabriel's eyes flickered with curiosity. "And your third wish?"

"I can't tell, because it's still in the making." My heart raced with unspoken hope that our relationship would blossom.

He laughed. "Well, I can't tell you my third wish either. By the way, isn't it interesting that we both had three wishes?"

"I hadn't thought of that. What were your other two wishes, if you care to share?"

"The first was that we'd continue to see each other, because I love spending time with you."

"What a sweet thing to say. I like you. What was your second wish?"

His eyes glittered. "After I told you how I met Jesus, that you'd still want to spend time with me."

"I want that even more now. I'm so glad we're together and that you survived. I think fate led us to each other." Electrical currents blissfully pulsed under my skin.

Gabriel stood and pulled me from the chair, his face shining with adoration. "God loves you, too, Evie. So much. He told me to tell you."

"Is that so?" My skin tingled with gratitude.

"Look at your life. You had a rough upbringing, but He took care of you. He made sure you got the job you wanted, and He brought Lou to you. He wanted her to take care of you, and she did. He knew you would reciprocate. He gave you your adorable home near this lake named Immanuel, which means 'God is here.' He knows how much you love Him." Gabriel's voice was steady, his gaze tender.

I beamed with delight. *God truly loves me. He can*

make anything happen. Well, almost anything. I wish Lou were still here with me.

Just then, my phone beeped with a text. A gasp escaped my lips.

"I've made it to the Other Side, and I'm so happy. I'll connect with you soon."

If you enjoyed *Heaven Sent*, please leave a review on your favorite platform.

ALSO BY MICHELLE ROMANO

Theo's Heart

Heaven Sent

Finding Faith

ABOUT THE AUTHOR

Michelle Romano is a gifted author whose stories are deeply rooted in faith, love, and the power of compassion. A devoted Christian and lifelong advocate for children, she writes with inspiration and purpose, offering hope to those facing hardships.

Her passion for fostering rescue dogs reflects her belief in second chances, which is a recurring theme throughout her books. Michelle's heartfelt storytelling draws readers into emotional journeys where grace prevails, wounds heal, and redemption is possible.

Inspired by her eclectic life experiences, she creates worlds where hearts mend and souls find their way. Her writing offers genuine comfort and encouragement, touching readers with its authenticity and enduring promise of renewal.

authormichelleromano.substack.com

amazon.com/author/michelleromano